CROCODILE TEARS

RAGHAV BADRINATH

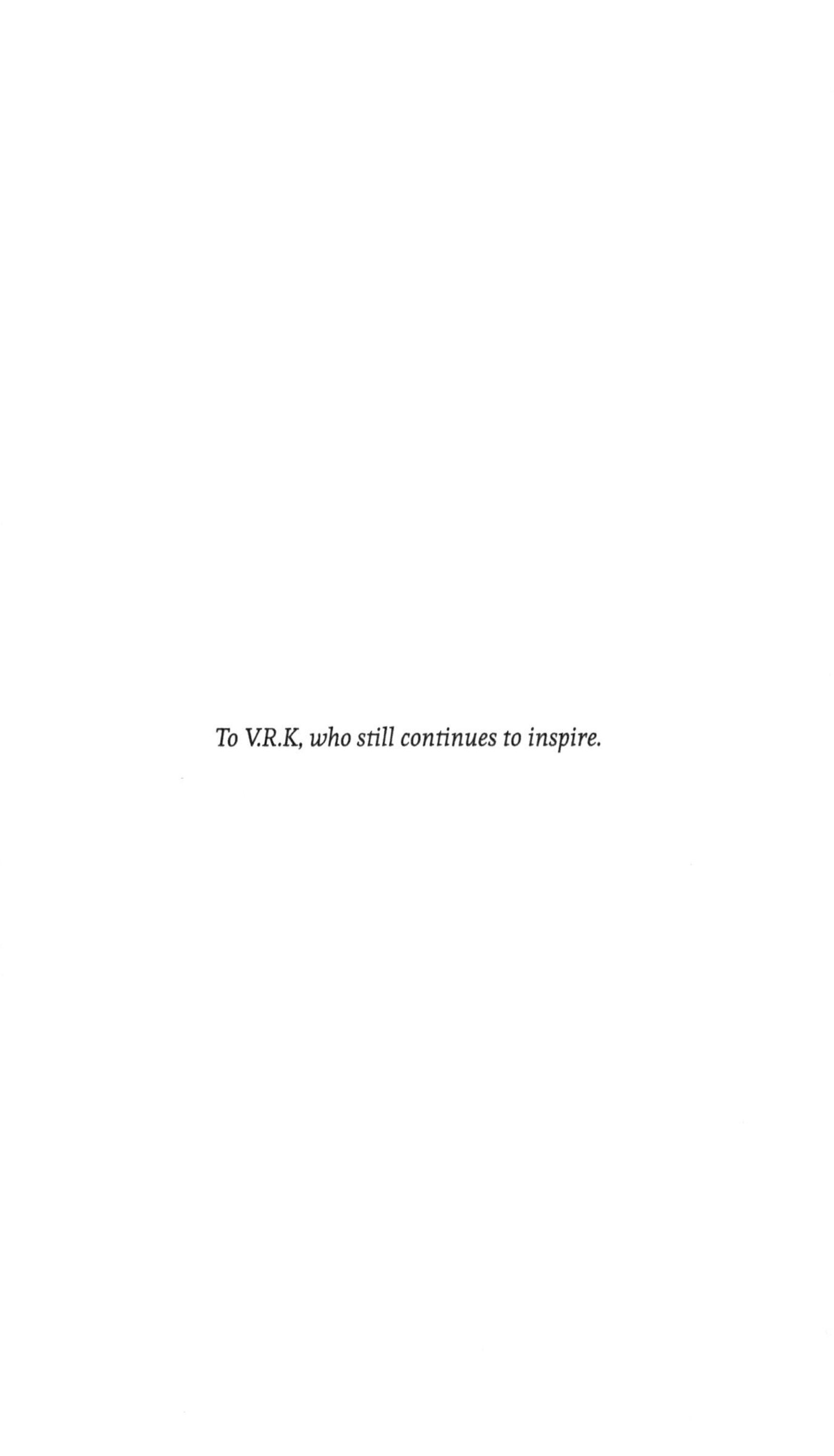

To V.R.K, who still continues to inspire.

Contents

Foreword

When the question of living forever had been posed, the rational person would often look at its side effects. They thought about how they would feel knowing that they were going to witness the full life of everyone around them. How they were going to see the lives of everyone around them end while they still hung around. How they would feel by attending the funeral of everyone around them, knowing that their own funeral will never take place. Destined to roam God's green Earth as a wanderer. Sick of watching everyone leave their life and move on to other phases of life. The people to whom the question had been posed, if given the opportunity, would often rashly accept the deal and decide to live forever. The same rational people would lose all humanity and see how the same people they cared for had moved on while they still forced to stay back. No strings need to be attached to such a situation. Why, the very idea itself was a burden that the human soul was not ready for.

ONE

It was 3 AM. Evan still didn't feel even the slightest hint of sleep. After half an hour or so of tossing and turning, he gave up, sitting straight on the damp mattress. He looked at the digital clock next to his bed. The LED screen wasn't telling him anything different. He sighed and made a mental note to throw away the large pack of estazolam buried in his closet.

He sighed again. Things were not going according to plan. He stood on legs that didn't feel quite there and made his way to the kitchen to grab a glass of orange juice. The idea of having a can of OJ at 3:30 AM made him feel slightly insane. Then again, he was supposed to be sleeping at 3:30 AM, so he supposed it didn't really matter anymore. Flexing his stiff shoulder, he made his way and opened the refrigerator. It was completely empty except for 4 slices of a week-old potpie, a few odd vegetables, and a can of orange juice well past its expiration date. "Let's hope at least that kills me finally" he murmured to himself as he pulled the can of orange juice took a box of a bland cereal placed in a shelf.

Knowing well enough that there wasn't any milk in the present nor will there be any for the foreseeable future, he poured the last bit of the stale cereal in a bowl and sat down at the chipped mahogany dining table. Eating the stale cereal dry and pouring the expired OJ into his mouth, he absently looked at the long crack zig-zagging through the wall opposite to the dining table. It was a very old home. He was tired of running and hiding. Juice dribbling down his chin, he looked at the ceiling.

He felt like screaming. With great difficulty he controlled himself.

"Please. Please take me with you"

he whispered to the ceiling. He tried to remember a time when life was simple. When it wasn't so complicated. He tried to remember times when he was aware of death and was obliged to recognise its presence breathing down his neck. He was sick of everything around him. He tried to remember his rather long past. It didn't come to him, only showing itself through bits and pieces he was terrified of. His entire life was a long blank which went on forever and had no past. It was just an enormous and never-ending slab of grey rock. He had lived a long life, a rather long one indeed, and it seemed to him that he wouldn't be able to escape whatever madness he was placed in. His life was what many people dreamed of and wrote about, longing for it in their darkest dreams, praying to every god for a chance to smack the hooded figure with the reaper in the bony face.

Everyone felt that they would be the one to finally beat death, the one to change fate and escape the claws of invisible shackles that bound everyone. It wasn't what it seemed. Evan was sick of it. He desperately begged for whatever god was left to let him rest. His past and future merged into a single pool. He remembered very less of his life. He only remembered how he was placed in such a situation. Oh yes. He remembered that with painfully clear clarity. It haunted him to snatch away whatever drifts of sleep he managed to get. For most people, the problem isn't resting. Oh who wouldn't want to rest. No. The real terror was never waking up. Oh how wretchedly he hoped to not wake up one day. Random flashes of what he had done floated into his mind, teasing and threatening to take away the last bit of sanity that remained. Evan didn't want to remember everything.

In fact, he didn't want to remember anything at all. Sleep, his only refuge, had also deserted him. Immortality was not all that it seemed. He wondered about other normal people who wished to live on forever. Oh how he envied the other mortals. He would DIE to have what they had. He didn't know for how long he had sat, looking at the cracked ceiling. Eventually, he managed to swallow the murk in his mouth. Licking his lips, he put his head down on the mahogany, his ink black hair making twirls in the surface of the table. He closed his eyes. Just like how the night had been, sleep had shown no sign of arriving. Instead, his mind wandered to what had been.

He thought about how he had managed to get himself in this mess in the first place. No sir, immortality was not at all what it had seemed. He stayed with his head bowed down on the mahogany until the sun rose.

TWO

A deep and painful tug in his gut awoke him. Evan barely had time to recognize the fact that he had managed to get some sleep, no matter how thin, when he sat bolt upright. The pain in his gut spread out throughout his body, sending long and hot needles of pain throughout. He ran towards the toilet, a dim part of him hoping it was something which would finally fulfull his wish of eternal sleep. It was not. He bent over the toilet when the murk of his horrendous breakfast came back up.

Wiping his mouth, head pounding, he sat back on his heels on the bathroom floor. He sat there swaying for how long he did not know. He eventually managed to gather himself up and stood. He looked at the bedside clock in his room. It was 9 AM already. He took a quick shower before pulling on his grub. Being alive for hundreds of years was no excuse to not work. He had to constantly be on the move so that people didnt become suspicious of the guy who looked 21 for the past decade. Evan had to learn this the hard way.

In his initial years, still in mourning and a sense of deep shock, he had seen how the people had looked at him when he still looked 21 when his wife had passed away. His son had been 50 years and his wife had died of old age. Even his own family had looked at him as though he were some spawn of the devil. Things had peaked when the villagers had burst into his house with flaming torches and pitch-forks. His son had led them.

Even upon his insistence they believed that he somehow held the "secret to immortality". When it became clear that Evan wouldn't share this grave "secret", they set fire to his house, while Evan was beaten and tied up to the large teak table inside. He somehow managed to escape with his life, and ran away from the town. From then, he learnt the lesson to never to be in a single town for too long. Evan still did not fully remember how he had gotten this special burden of being far from death, but one thing he made a note of was how the people around him reacted when they saw the quality in a man.

Another thing that Evan made a note of was how he felt older after his wife, Annie, had died. Evan wasn't sure how he knew, but he knew nonetheless. He felt it. He had grown a year older. According to his calculations, he was 24 years old now. Everyday of the past 200 or so years had taken its brunt on him. Around the past 50 years, the pressure had grown on him, taking away parts of his mind and soul, leaving him with loneliness and despair.

First had come the crushing sorrow of watching all his loved ones die. He had attended the funeral of his parents and his first wife, eventually driven out of the village. He had secretly returned to witness the funeral of his own first son. The initial crowd of people who had set fire to his house and called him a "vampire", were either dead themselves or were old who no longer remembered who they were. In any case, very few remained those who knew. He had managed to spy on his grandson, who had grown to look just like his father, and 2 kids standing next to their father who Evan had assumed were his great-grandkids. He had struggled on with the sorrow for the next 20 years and had managed to bury it deep within himself. However, those memories still came back to haunt him in the depths of his darkest nightmares. Next had come the equally harsh loneliness he had to deal with as he drifted in and out of various towns and through 2 world wars.

Evan had briefly considered the idea of joining the army. However, the notion of providing the government details of the fact that he was born a good 100 years before the present age seemed like something that would get him in trouble. Unable to procure and provide other details and records, Evan had dropped the idea of signing up for the army. Over his long and unintentional wanderlust, he had met several people and had become quite close to them, and he had been with them for a long period of time, running away from the region when he sensed that the others were becoming suspicious of the guy who was young for many years. In most of the small towns that Evan had stayed in, it had been the same.

First rumours were created by annoyingly observant people, floated around as a mere speculation, as it grew support and spread like a wildfire. It then went on as the murmurs and whispers among the people grew when they saw him, some even pointing at him behind his back. The next stage was what Evan had nicknamed the "religion phase". It was when religion was taken in a rather sloppy fashion as the common people became convinced that Evan was "a vampire" or a "spawn from the depths of the Earth" or a ghost. At the religious phase, all people were on edge and restless, waiting for an opportunity to take action on the rumours which they felt were the "Will of the god himself". It required little encouragement for the people to suddenly decide to painfully relieve the "ghost", who had the gift of immortality, of his life.

Many people had assumed that Evan somehow held the gift and secret to the path of immortality. Over his life, people had begged, bribed, flattered, and even tried to threaten him into making them immortal. Evan almost forgotten his life before he became released from the slippery holds of death, much less remember how he had managed to do it. His responses to the people who accused him of living forever had been apologetic and pleading. If anything, he was tired of it. He was sick of watching every person he ever loved in the course of his life ultimately meet their end. He supposed he was not sick of the people around him dying since he had managed to push the anguish down to the deepest parts of his soul which were no longer given thought. No.

He knew that he was sick of himself since he felt that when each person around him ultimately met their end, he had sooner or later felt himself gain one more year. He knew that as long as he was still stuck in his early twenties, his body was capable of regenerating and fighting against every disease he had run into. His body was still young. It was capable of living forever. Evan wanted to rest as soon as possible and he knew that the only way for that to happen was if he became an old man.

At the age of 60, he knew that he would be more susceptible to diseases, ultimately heralding in the long awaited reaper. No indeed. He was sick of himself for watching him just gain just one year as each person who he had considered close to him finally met their end.

What he found repugnant was the fact that he wished for it to happen.

THREE

He jogged from his apartment, leaping over the rickety stairs of the old building. Evan had managed to somehow get the house, given a large part of his measly income for rent. He could not afford a vehicle and given his forever-nomadic movement across America, he felt that he didn't need a vehicle. Not to mention that they didn't make cars like they made it a 100 years ago. He had managed to never learn to drive. Muttering under his breath, he walked the 4 miles to the Samsons' All You Can Buy, where he worked on weekdays for the $9.52 per hour. He was able to make it to work in half an hour. He rushed in to his spot, managing to wear the bright Green cap of the Samsons store before he got yelled at by Dave, the store manager.

He went to booth number 4 and sat down, re-directing some of the rush to his stall. He worked quietly, checking and billing each product of the customer. After the first 4 people or so had paid and made their way to leave the store, James from the stall beside, peeked over and waved to Evan. James had found Evan to be a rather queer person. For starters, Evan spoke differently, with a rather musty accent lingering over his inconsistent English. Like his mother had often told him, James had often believed that the eyes were the windows to the soul within a person.

For him, looking into the eyes of Evan had been a source of unending confusion, thus he made a point to do it every time. Today however, Evan looked more bedraggled than usual. His eyes were bloodshot and his white blonde hair was messed up as though he had just stumbled through a tornado to work. His uniform was scuffed and dirty, with the ridiculously large and bright green Samsons cap hanging askew on his crown. James had never asked the boy's age, but he felt that Evan was somewhere in his early twenties. Seeing the guy depressed and alone, with no one to talk to, James had made every opportunity to talk to the kid, who he thought looked much older than his 20-something years. As always, James looked right into the kid's startlingly blue eyes, once again deeply perplexed.

It had seemed to James as if some un-namable and deadly beast was locked up inside those dark circles of his pupils, surrounded by the ocean of blue of the iris, destined to be imprisoned forever. He felt as if the boy's soul held something more deeper, barely in control under his vague and unassuming outlook. James chided himself mentally. "No" he whispered. He wasn't perplexed by what those eyes held. He was downright scared by what the boy held, always on the edge.

"Goodmornin'" said James, his voice clearing the boy enough to make him look straight at James. As usual, when their eyes met, James felt a second of paralysing fear shaking his bones, then it was replaced by a feeling of confusion yet again. "Morning" came the reply from the kid. James shuffled his feet, as if he were some misbehaving called to the principal. Aware of what he was doing, he stopped and made himself look at the bedraggled kid again. "I was just wondering if you could come to have some lunch with the rest of the guys for some steak at the place on the corner of Redhill ave.".

Evan just looked at James for a few seconds, and smiled. The smile made him looked a hundred years younger. James immediately relaxed. The boy replied, "Sure thing" and James let out a breath he had been holding in for quite some time, unbeknownst to himself. James just smiled back and after some more chatter, made his way back to his booth. The customers were starting to pile in again and the last thing that he wanted was to get yelled at by the store manager, a big bulky man who did not hesitate to relieve people of their job. The other guys who came with him for lunch were initially annoyed at James' proposal to invite the quiet kid.

They felt that he would ruin the mood. James was adamant however. He had wanted to know what the boy was hiding so very deeply within, and what else was there to make the tongue loose other than taking the guy to a hearty steak dinner at the so-called "Best restaurant in town"? Moreover, James was curious. "Tonight's going to be fun" he muttered to himself, smiling at the old lady who had just bought a basket full of green vegetables. "Do you need a carry-on bag with that madam?" Oh yes.

Tonight was going to be very fun indeed.

FOUR

Howie was in hiding. What had first started as a harmless prank had quickly turned deadly serious. Howie was just playing around when he pushed the first Wesley brother. It wasn't his fault that Howie had just hit the little boy a little too hard and the kid had fallen from the top of a bridge, falling into the fast and dark moving Dominguez channel.It had not helped that the bridge was 6 feet above the water-level. Oh and the endless screeching that Arthur had sounded immediately afterwards on seeing his twin brother fall from a bridge. It was more of a favour for Howie to help their parents by also shoving Arthur from the bridge. Because who wanted to be left with one when you had originally had two?

Hey, Howie had been that one who was left behind when his own brother had died in a motorcycle crash. That would have been hard on the parents indeed. No, what Howie had done had been perfectly correct. Why was he just helping other people? Then it occurred to him that hey, maybe those pestering little kids hadn't been dead and maybe they were alive. How bothersome it would be if they told something to an adult about the good ol' Howie? About the little howie who had been delivering newspapers from the age of 10? The howie who had once shot that relentless pug on the rothermans' house which had bit him once when he was delivering the papers at 5 in the morning?

No. No one had ever put it back to good old howie. No. Howie, who was 21 years old and never managed to finish highschool before dropping out after threatening the principal. Not the howie who was a slightly mentally "dysfunctional" as the doctors said it but a good lad indeed. No. Howie wouldn't let the boys go and blab to all the people. No sir. Howie was gonna take care of them both. And he did take care of them.

That had been a week ago. It was found out that Howie had something to do with those brutal killings when they saw him emerge later from the banks of the Dominguez channel and walk down to the city, bleeding from various scratches on his face from what looked suspiciously like deep scratches from nails. With many witnesses claiming strongly that they had indeed seen a "long butcher knife which was dripping with a red substance which looked "suspiciously like blood". Howie knew that the police was after him.

He had not done anything. No officer. He had just been playing. Oh yes. He knew that if they police caught him they would take him back to the correctional center.And howard didn't want to go there. No. So he ran. He took old man Luther Kingsley's car for a ride away from Torrance and its people, after hitting the man in the back of the head. Howie had told sorry to the unconscious man.

Luther wouldn't say anything to anyone. Howie took the rusty chevy pickup and drove towards Long beach. No one was going to catch howie.

No sir. Howie was one lucky ducky.

FIVE

Howie knew well enough to keep within the speed limit. He didnt have any cash on him. Since it was late at night already, Howie didnt face much trouble. He kept the window cracked open with the radio softly playing "Whole lotta love" by Led zeppelin. Howie didnt care much for the music but he needed something to take his mind off of things. He knew that when he got upset or excited, he often made rash decisions.

Under other circumstances, Howie would have been just fine with doing whatever he felt like doing, but this time however, he felt that he had to make careful decisions. For that he had to look and act normal. For once, for reasons he couldnt explain, howie felt that it VERY important that he didnt get caught. Yes sir indeed. So howie increased the volume of the radio until the old chevy was booming music with led zeppelin exclaiming that he was gonna give every inch of his love.

Howie plastered a broad and fake smile on his face, the yellow teeth on full display, and fixed his eyes on the road in front of him. Howie had decided that long beach was too close to home. He knew the police force was slow but even they wouldnt have trouble finding howie. Instead, Howie pushed on, deciding to move past Long island and instead move further away. For now he felt that San diego would be an appropriate spot to lay low for a couple of days before he made his way out of the state.

Pushing an even speed, the smile wider than ever, Howie moved along, alone on the road except for the radio. Now it had moved from Led Zeppelin to Jack Harlow singing about how hes vanilla. No sir Howie was just the regular joe who loved music and certainly had nothing to do with those two "accidents"at torrance. No sir, the police were not behind him. He still had time in his hands. Not to mention a whole lotta blood too.

It was a full half hour later that he realised that the old chevy was rapidly running out of gas. Howie had had his eyes fixed on the road, his mind wandering away. It was by pure accident that his eyes had somehow drifted to the dash and he had seen the red light blinking, indicating low fuel. Howie wasnt happy. He wanted to be comfortably halfway to San Diego before the end of the night. Instead, he was going to have to stop at some small town barely 50 miles away from torrance. Nonetheless, he reluctantly kept is eyes on the road around him.

He did so after slamming the radio a few times before switching it off for good measure as it rambled on. He looked at the cracked dial of his wristwatch, its glass broken and its face spattered with blood, and saw that it was already a quarter past 10. Most shops were closed at this time and god knew if Howie would manage to find a gas station in this deserted little town.

Grudgingly he agreed with himself to stop for the night. Now the next issue was to find a good place to park the chevy before he could lay his hands on a better ride. Then it occurred to him that he didn't even know where he was right now. The chevy low on fuel slowly crawled past streets, making its way past the closed shutters of different stores.

All Howie was looking was for a place to just park the Chevy under shade. He knew that he couldn't afford to get a room at some cheesy motel, given that he didn't have any cash on him, and the fact that he didn't really think anyone would give him a room after seeing his shirt magenta in the colour of dried blood and splatters of it all over his arms.

Well he didn't expect them to give him the room then not blab about it. "Those people are not in the right state of mind" he murmured to himself. His own voice surprised him. He started laughing, quietly at first, becoming a loud cackle as he imagined all those people who had said that about him. Oh how wrong they were. Howie was a good boy. He was gonna show it to everyone too. He found an empty clearing beside a row of posh suburban houses. Howie checked a few times to make sure that no one was watching him. No sir, all the lights in those houses were switched off.

Only the faces of darkened houses looked at him. He was finally, completely, free. The thought of how fun his evening had set Howie off again. He parked the car, almost out of gas, near an empty clearing in the forest, directly perpendicular to the darkened houses. Still giggling silently to himself, Howie walked deeper and deeper into the forest, careful not to step on any broken branches or leaves. Once he felt he had gone deep enough, Howie sat next down heavily next to a rock jutting on the ground. With his back leaning against the tree, Howie closed his eyes. He felt like sleeping now.

SIX

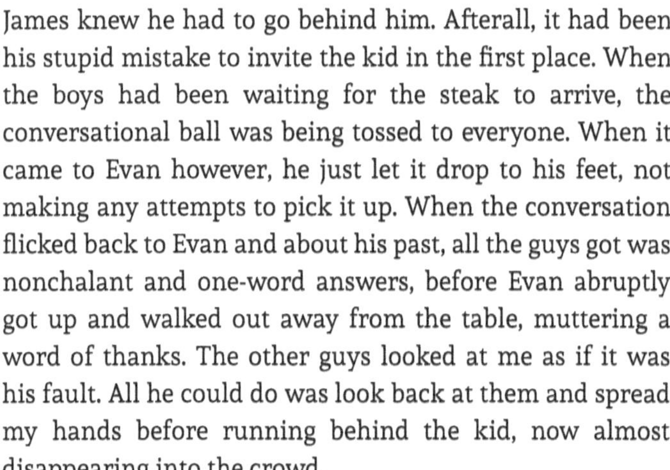

James knew he had to go behind him. Afterall, it had been his stupid mistake to invite the kid in the first place. When the boys had been waiting for the steak to arrive, the conversational ball was being tossed to everyone. When it came to Evan however, he just let it drop to his feet, not making any attempts to pick it up. When the conversation flicked back to Evan and about his past, all the guys got was nonchalant and one-word answers, before Evan abruptly got up and walked out away from the table, muttering a word of thanks. The other guys looked at me as if it was his fault. All he could do was look back at them and spread my hands before running behind the kid, now almost disappearing into the crowd.

Evan was having a hell of a headache. It was the kind of headache that made you crawl up into a ball and wish for it to go away. Thankfully, Evan had had enough experience to know when such a headache was usually about to come, like the calm before a storm, and Evan was sure was well going to get as far away from the storm as possible before it hit. The relentless quartet of questions from the annoying guys sitting opposite to him and not helped his state of mind.

To be honest, the only reason Evan had come in the first place was so that he could enjoy a decent bite of steak. He hadnt had those in centuries. And with Evan, you can bet that he meant what he said when he said "hadnt had those in centuries". He kept his head bent low as he made out of the crowded restaurant. "Well, so much for a good meal." he muttered to himself, the headache increasing from an incessant and dull thud to a more sharper and heavier throbbing. 'All the telltale signs' Evan talked out loud to himself, emerging into th deserted and darkened redhill ave street. Not a car was in sight.

He sighed again, going back through his mental inventory of what he thought was at that crumbling mess he called his house. James just came out of the crowded restaurant and jogged over to Evan, who had his head bent low as if he were looking at the ground for gold coins. James called out to the kid almost melting into the darkness. Evan evidently jumped, being startled from his thoughts. He turned over to look at James jogging over to him. Evan was having trouble remember things before the past 50 years, but he supposed he had broken some sort of internal record by staying in this place for this long.

He had been living in Orange County for almost 30 years now, the fact which was possible by Evan working in many different places and industries, from factories to hotels, barely drawing attention to himself. He kept telling himself he had to dye his hair to some normal colour like brown from its original white-blond, so that people wouldnt remember him. Evan had found out that people tended to ignore things for a surprisingly long amount of time, being engrossed in their own mortal lives to see about what was happening all around them.

He had remarked to himself, not once, that these people wouldnt know God if he was standing right before them. So keen to run on their mortal lives, running towards their goal, irrationally hoping that somehow they would be able to do so forever. Most of mortal people wished to live on forever, but Evan knew how excruciatingly painful it was. He would trade his life with any mortal in a heartbeat, if ever given the choice. You dont live forever by escaping the reaper forever. You live forever by living your own life to the fullest. Most mortals didnt seem to get that. In this stage of Evan's life, James had been one (if not only) of the ones who seemed to understand.

The guy had a little twinkle in his eyes, that suggested maybe he just understand what Evan was going through and just maybe may even be able to help him. He didnt want to fight with the one person whom he called a friend. He didnt want to get more attached than that. He was well aware of the situation that befell people he held close to his heart. That sort of loneliness did take a heavy toll on his life. Evan turned to look back at James.

'Hey man you good?' James asked. 'Yeah just not in the mood for dinner right now' Evan replied, steadily meeting James' eyes.

He was seemingly unaware of the effect that had on people. James looked on and decided that enough was enough. He had always grown to help people in need, and James, like his mother, had the gift of insight. He was almost always able to guess how people felt.

His mother used to jokingly call him, "The Emperor of Empathy" and James had done all but agree. An internal sense told him that now it was time for him to actually ask his friend and understand what he was going through. Because James was sure there was something buried deep under the weary personality, and those deep blue eyes. Yes something indeed.

"Hey look Evan, I know there is something bothering you. Yes you try very hard to hide it but i know it. It always helps when you talk about things like this. Its ok. You can tell me-" but james was cut off by the echo of a loud car. By instinct, Evan grabbed James and pulled him into an alley right behind the restaurant as an old and rusted chevy pickup went past them, the radio blaring some popular song James had heard of before but didnt know the name.

He watched with a growing sensation of unease as the pickup slowly crawled past them, the driver hunched over the wheel, and looking at all directions around him. For reasons James didnt understand, sweat had broken all over him and he was dead scared. He looked on as beads of sweat of poured over his face. He couldnt even make himself look at Evan, who was right beside him. No. For some reason unbeknownst to himself, he felt that even turning his head to look would set the driver of the rusty chevy off. Set him off to do what? He was just another guy who had wandered by mistake into this small city, not some demon from the underworld.

However, the more he tried to reason with himself, he found himself still standing, frozen. It was only for a few seconds but it felt like an eternity as the pickup slowly crawled forward, blaring the song "Selfish" by Justin Timberlake to the empty buildings. It's insane what the mind decides to remember in such situations. James slowly relaxed and later felt a bit silly for being terrified of an old guy in a pickup. James finally turned to look at Evan, who was deadly still. He looked back at James and motioned his hands forward. James knew what the lunatic next to him was suggesting. Even though his rational mind had no trouble with the suggestion, his body was inwardly screaming.

He was terrified but he nonetheless nodded. Evan had just suggested that they follow the chevy. James wasn't sure what it was, but there was something that made the hairs on the nape of his neck stand straight up. It was like listening to the grating of a sharp and large rock on a blackboard,the sound amplified by 4 speakers right next to him. His heart pounding, James followed Evan as they trailed the crawling chevy.The beat was still echoing down the empty street as the car moved forward until it was just a tiny speck to the eyes of james.

James didn't want to ask it out loud but he knew the answer nonetheless.

The driver of the chevy had been grinning broadly, his shirt covered with dried blood.

SEVEN

James didnt know for how long he had been following the car. His legs were throbbing and he felt the urge, more than once, to ditch Evan and run away back to the restaurant. He could just as well go back, eat his cold steak, talk to the guys and go home, forgetting all this ever happened. However, as much as he wanted to go back, he was also very intrigued by what he had seen. No. Deep down, he felt a much more primary and more powerful emotion of curiosity. Out loud, it may have seemed insensitive but to his own mind, it was perfectly reasonable.

James was curious about the blood on that guy's shirt. He wasn't able to see the driver's face fully, but he had seen that wide and glaring smile, those yellow teeth sticking out. All of james' attention was taken up by that bloody shirt. James was so lost in his thoughts that he didnt realise Evan had stopped. His eyes on the ground and his mind left free to wander, James kept going forward until he collided into Evan. He turned around to look at James, annoyed. They were crouching behind a big Escalade, peering around as the rusty pickup grounded to a halt in front of a large clearing in the forest, opposite to the large suburban houses, now darkened. Even though it was fully dark, James' eyes quickly adjusted to the darkness. He could make out the tiny circle of the driver, looking to both sides of him to make sure there was no one looking at him. From a distance, James watched as the tiny bobble-head once more looked to both sides then finally switched off the engine. James had no idea what they were doing standing there. Ok so what if it was a mass-murderer?

America had seen enough of those. The right thing to do was to dial 911 and inform the police, not playing Sherlock Holmes with a very dangerous man. James opened his mouth as if to say just that to Evan but before he could even utter a word, Evan held up a finger to his lips. His eyes were glittering in the dark. James was confused but then he heard it. Interspersed amongst the low muttering was a small chuckle, as if he were laughing at a good-natured joke at the dinner table. It abruptly hit a crescendo, blasting the eerily quiet neighbourhood with a wave of screeching, ending just as abruptly as it had started. James was terrified to even look at the guy in the pickup. He instead looked at his sneakers with renewed attention. James heard the door of the chevy slam. He looked up, instinctively rather than by will, and looked at the guy with his head bent down at a queer angle. He didn't even bother to lock the car before walking into the entry of the dark passageway into the forest. Gravel crunched under his boots as he walked deeper inside until he was fully out of view for james. The low chuckling slowly became fainter and fainter until it wasn't heard at all. Evan instinctively moved forward, as if he wanted to follow the creepy guy into the forest. James was too tired.

Without uttering a single word, he stood up, and grabbed Evan's arm, roughly pulling him to his feet. Looking straight ahead, James dragged him back towards the steakhouse. Evan didnt struggle back. Just sparing one look behind him, to look at the strange crevice in the unassuming wall of the forest which had swallowed up a killer, James increased his pace. The roads were fully deserted. Neither of them uttered a single word. They both were lost in their own worlds as their legs carried them back to the restaurant, feeling faint and dim to their minds which were far away. James managed to come out of his stupor just to mumble softly,"You cannot run behind the boogeyman into the forest at night". A voice deep within James told him that things were about to get way worse, way fast. To this, James could only readily agree

EIGHT

Howie was no stranger to nightmares. They occasionally caused him to wake up at 2 AM, in most cases, after which he wouldnt be able to sleep the rest of the night. Thanks to the meds he was told to take by the psychiatrist assigned to him, these occurrences were very less. This time however, he had had to deal with many things and the least important of all his worries was to remember to take his meds. Oh well. He was getting sick of them anyway. It had probably been for the best. It didnt help things that howie despised Dr. John, his psychiatrist, who insisted on having a "talk" with howie for an hour every week, talking about how he felt and what his thoughts were.

Whatever his faults may be, Howie wasnt stupid. He knew that getting a "talk" by the local psychiatrist was code for stating that Howie was indeed, not "mentally alright 'up there". It had infuriated him. He was normal. Howie KNEW that he was a more "normal" human than any of the doctors he had ever been forced to met. Being called mentally unstable was something which had also infuriated his mother, who had to raise little Howie all by herself as her husband just woke up one day and choose to go away. Closing his eyes and leaning his head on the wide trunk of the tree, Howie tried to get some sleep but it kept escaping from his desperate grasp.

Eventually, after a long time, where howie felt as if back had just been cemented to stay in the same position, he finally managed to drift away, his aching body feeling more farther away and fainter as he slipped into sleep.

Howie felt very awake. He suddenly felt a stab of pain in his legs. He tried to say something but he felt as if his tongue had swollen to the size of a balloon, covering his mouth, and preventing him from speech. He looked down an saw that he was kneeling, his legs chained by a huge rusty chain, twisting all around his body until his chest. His greasy hair hung in his eyes, making him blink rapidly in annoyance. Something told howie that something was amiss. He felt it. Something was not right. Other than his own chained body, everything was covered in a heavy blanket of darkness. Howie felt strangely claustrophobic, his neck and shoulders suddenly prickly and itchy, as if it had just been taken as a nest for a horde of red ants.

He twisted his neck, desperately trying in vain to say something, anything. A major part for the heavy sensation of fear for howie was not only the fact that he was tied. No sir. It was because howie sensed something waiting for him in the darkness. Some beast lurking in the shadows of his own mind, looking at him, chained and writhing. The itchy sensation in his neck abruptly aggravated. Howie was twisting his head in all directions, as if he were being electrocuted.

Finally a cold and deep voice whispered, "Hiya howie". Howard felt the blood in face drain out, leaving his face devoid of colour and giving him a pasty complexion. The itchy and prickly sensation in the nape of his neck also abruptly stopped. He stopped twisting his head and looked into the darkness where he felt the voice had come from, but in reality, he had no idea where the voice had come from. It seemed it had just come from all around, as if we were standing inside the thing. Howie couldn't even manage a response, even though now he felt that he could speak if he wanted to. In response however, all he could manage was a whimper.

"Dear old boyyy" the voice murmured again, its voice barely above a whisper, but still perfectly heard. Howie's heart stopped cold. This what his mother had called him before. Before her de- "How are you doing old boy?" it whispered again, the voice growing slightly above a whisper.

Before Howard could even think of a response, the voice boomed out, "I said, HOW ARE YOU DOING". It reverbated all around him, thundering into his eardrums as he tumbled from his knees to flat down on the floor, his nose connecting hard with whatever the floor was made of. Howie could sense the ferocity and intensity, almost destroying his sanity. His knees were tied together but that still didn't stop him from involuntarily shaking them from fear. His ears still ringing, a part of him dimly noticed that tears were pouring down his eyes. "Alright lets move to business" the deep voice purred.

"We both know what happens to people who tell everyone that you are sick right?" it murmured.

Howie nodded his head in response, his eyes wide and terrified. He feigned confusion but he knew well enough what this voice was speaking of. Oh yes. He knew. "Now howie, what would you do if i told you that there was still someone out there, who genuinely believe that you are still sick?"

Howie didnt respond. He spent 5 years in various rehab centres and institutions. He was tortured and bullied into not ever taking this bait. But yet, as the voice purred on,

Howie felt himself drawn. He slowly forgot about the horrors he had faced. He forgot about the prickly feeling, the pain in his body, the anxiety and the claustrophobia. He listened to the voice.

He listened closely. "Let me tell you something howie-boy, there is someone out there, someone still out to go to the police. Someone whos going to take to you back to the institution." Howie knew this wasn't true, but yet, he felt himself believing every word. "And what if, just what if, this someone is the person who is responsible for what happened to your mother?"

Howie was just crying harder now. "Tell me howard, if anyone had the ability to prevent death himself and still choose not to save other kind people like your mother, are those people not murderers? Are they not the criminals who have to be locked in institution rather than you?" the words just washed over howie. He was getting tired now. "Evan Stevenson, Charlie Wittaker, Rodney Davis, Theodore Stapleton. He has taken countless names as he roamed the Earth for thousands of years, escaping death and living forever."

Howard felt a wave of nausea. "An apostle from the underworld, a mistake of God. He is right here, conniving and planning to send you back to the loonybin. He is always gathering the people against you, Howie. You cannot go to another institution. No sir. No. You have to find this..creature and you have to end him. You have to hand him over to death. Only then will the scales be balanced and your mother can rest in peace." Howie wasn't sure how the death of his mother had anything to do with this "apostle" but a deep part within him insisted that he was the reason the scales were unbalanced, and that he was the reason his mother was so cruelly taken away. It was all his fault.

What was his name? Oh yes, Evan Stevenson. Howie was going to find him. Howie was going to make sure the scales were balanced. In a way, he was going after a killer. A murderer who had been responsible for the death of his mom. "Yes Howie. Hand him over to death and you will finally feel peace. Kill him and you will be forever safe. Kill him and the police will not come after you. Kill him…and you may live forever".

Howie jolted up from sleep. His body still ached and his mind was racing. He was momentarily confused about where he was. He looked around. He was asleep on the trunk of a tree. The sun was shining through the tall trees, and he could hear the sound of a stream passing through. "Just a nightmare. Nothing else. Just-" and howie froze. He felt the area near his knees and saw that it was scarred. Covered in brownish flakes and with deep grooves along his white skin. Almost as if..his legs had been chained together. Howie shook his head. This was ridiculous. It was just a nightmare. Nothing more. Even if it had somehow been true, he already had 2 murders on his hands.

He was not going to kill another random person because a voice in his dream said so. He was not. But deep within, Howie knew that he was going to do exactly as the voice had said. It had to be done. He had to right the wrongs. No one could be allowed to remain alive eternally. No one except God himself. In a way, this guy had killed Howie's mother. He shook himself again. He needed some time to think. A distant tug at the base of the brain nudged him. It was the origin of a monstrous headache. Howie hadnt had those since the time he had been locked for 2 years at the institution of the mentally ill.

They had only occurred when he had been taking those awful meds. But he had long since stopped taking them because they always left him impulsive and on edge. Yet that was exactly how he was feeling right now. "I just need some time"he mumbled to himself and managed to struggle to his feet after two attempts. Making his way towards the sound of flowing water, his hands brushed across his face. His fingers returned wet. His cheeks were damp and covered with moisture.

As if he had been crying. His eyes widened. "Evan stevenson "a voice muttered at the base of his mind.

It was the same voice.

NINE

Evan and James walked side-by-side back toward the way they had come from, until they reached the diner where they had both run out on a meal of steak. Oh how long ago that incident seemed to James, even though it had only happened less than an hour before. They both stood outside the diner, now slowly quieting down as more and more people left the restaurant. James no doubt knew that his friends were still inside, eating their steak and jostling with each other, completely oblivious as a mass murderer just casually strolled into town, singing along to the radio.

No. Their major concern at the moment would have been regarding whether if indeed the steak sitting before them on their plates was the medium rare they had ordered, or god forbid, a well-done steak had been given and the greatest conspiracy of the twentieth century was unfolding right before their eyes. James envied their ignorance. He wanted that to be his main concern, not the worry of whether a killer was roaming loose into the city. James supposed that it was the work of the police and they would catch the psycho before dawn. A part of James' mind was just content with the fact that the police were definitely around here somewhere and they would do what was required.

No one had asked for the help of the generous skinny-almost-scrawny James. No sir. But the thought that a mass murderer was somewhere close, watching everyone's movements, was gnawing at the base of his brain. He had just assumed that the lunatic he had seen in the car to be a mass-murderer and something told James that he wasn't wrong. He turned to look at Evan, standing beside him, almost blending with the shadows, if not for the blob of floating whitish-blond hair. Evan was looking into the diner. James couldn't exactly see Evan's face but again he just assumed it was Evan's usual look.

The jaw clenched, and the eyes looking straight ahead. His face adorned with a stone-like expression of indifference. One would just move past such a person had not the said person decide to look into Evan's eyes. Those deep blues which looked like the well of the world, filled with sheets of water, stretching endlessly within the mirage of the inner boundaries of the well. James suddenly felt angry. He wouldn't have had to witness the lunatic screaming along to the radio then going for a stroll within the forest if not for Evan.

Evan who couldn't even talk to his friends and had stormed out when they asked him where he had been working before. It infuriated James. He would have been very well off without having been burdened by such unnecessary information. He spun towards Evan, a hot torrent of words rising in his chest, but they were instantly smothered when he looked at Evan. He wasn't looking into the restaurant now. He was looking dead into James' eyes, and involuntarily, James flinched but still made eye contact.

Evan's face looked like the perfect human equivalent for the proverb, "A goose walked over my grave". A part of James thought that if his expression had been put on a board next to the phrase, people would have no trouble whatsoever trying to understand the origin and true meaning of the proverb. James' feet grew cold under his shoes. Evan muttered, barely above a whisper, "He knows". James raised his eyebrows questioningly in response, but a part of him already knew the answer. It was in the group of thoughts that one would seriously pondering as reality at around 2 AM, after having woken up from a particularly nasty nightmare.

As the day slowly progressed however, one would forget all about the nightmare, only having been left with the slimy residue, scattered throughout the brain, which randomly popped into existence on random moments. Little did anyone know that humans were only close to being a supreme being only at those times, having woken up from such a nightmare.

It was at that point, when the brain was fueled with imagination and stimulus, and the mind was placed teetering on the brink of madness and disbelief, that the mind was directly open to communication to other highly evolved and supreme beings. It was the closest that human beings had ever gotten to being a God. A shame it had been left as little puddles on the floor of the brain, as humans continued on with their meaningless work, somehow feeling that the money would be all they need to truly become immortal. James blinked twice.

Evan muttered again, "He knows and soon he will be coming after him. Oh he knows." Without even waiting for a reply, Evan dashed into the darkness, running headfirst into shadows. James couldn't follow. He had always known that there was something that was rather peculiar about the kid who had worked with him. But he had no idea what it was or how profound it may be.

Even though James didn't want to accept what his mind was yammering to him, like driving a baseball bat home on the windshield of a car repeatedly, he suddenly didn't know anymore.

He didn't even want to acknowledge the thoughts that were blasting through his mind, questioning his reality.

James was suddenly *very very scared.*

TEN

Evan grunted awake. He sat up bolt upright in his little cot with the stained mattress. A part of him was pleasantly surprised to know that he had actually managed to fall asleep even though he had repeatedly failed at the same task repeatedly on several occasions. He stretched, his tight back crackling as he struggled to recall what had transpired on the night before. As queer as it sounded to himself, for a moment, he could not for the life of him remember how he had come back to his house, much less remember the protocol for achieving humongous feats like falling asleep.

Then it slowly came back to him, in distorted bits and pieces. His new-found cheery outlook for the day soon turned bleak when he remembered the mysterious pickup rumbling into town, and the immediate response of his mind when he looked at the lunatic. Over Evan's rather long life, he had come to trust dearly his intuitions. The so-called "developed" and "modern" people scoffed at intuition but they were yet unaware as intuition was deep rooted into the mechanism of man. The primary human relied fully on intuition as his intelligence and memory was still in a process of development.

Evan was around when people initially claimed rightfully that intuition was part of the human brain that was beyond the discovery of scientists, a subtle yet essential isle, developed much beyond its time, crammed in an insignificant wedge of a self-righteous species prone to forget its past. At the moment, Evan's foreign brain was in overdrive, his mind pumping a clear message of danger. Even though he was perfectly normal a moment ago, he felt his palms becoming greasy and oily, his heart beating double-time, and the skin of hands and legs erupt in gooseflesh.

He knew what he needed to do. He was well aware of what was happening. Everyone was subject to the calling of the earth, as it slowly yet powerfully pulled the human race back into its surface, freeing them of the illusion that they were a species self-made. This calling was the same for all. Some people may be called upon earlier than their expectations were fulfilled, but it will still take them. The messenger of the earth, in the form of death, comes knocking to take the rich and poor alike.

To be exempted from such a process would appear at first that the earth was indeed prejudiced. It was granting a supreme boon to a man, who may or may not be worthy. The messenger dared not to fetch such a person's soul. But yet, the earth called, however slowly but steadily, to a fundamental aspect of the body. Evan did not remember much about his long past, other than the previous half-decade, but remembered that no matter who is exempted from such an undertaking, nature did not work that way.

Life is not prejudiced, contrary to anyone's notions. An event akin had last happened when Evan was coming to terms with his relatively newfound immortality, seeing with deep anguish as he lost his first family, and soon being turned out of the town with pitchforks and blazing torches after the reports of the man "free of death" was roaming among them. Evan managed to just barely escape with his life. Even though this event was bound to happen countless times over his everlasting life, this event really stuck with him. This was why, even after he had forgotten almost everything about his past, he still vividly remembered the details of the event.

It was not because this was the first occurrence. It was because the people had not realised that a man of immortality was living among them, but the people had been made aware explicitly about the same. Granted, the people were bound to notice eventually, the event was different. The people did not gradually realise the reality about Evan. No sireee. He was very publicly flayed. Castigated and admonished to such extent that it yanked the attention of everyone.

Evan was criminated by a particular person. Memories of the same was exploding in his mind, yammering at him to run away right now. He had just managed to escape with his life, his immortality almost lost. Evan knew the power of that beast. He knew that it was just the earth's way of scoffing at his athanasia, angered at someone escaping fate. So compelled to take action that it had sent a spawn of the underworld to extract the soul living past its due.

His blood turned ice cold as that face, fresh as ever, came back in his mind. He was terrified. He knew that the Earth had sent someone yet again to bring him back to where he was meant to be. He felt terrified as it was the same face that he had seen yesterday in the pickup truck, covered in blood, grinning wildly. A broad smile plastered to its face as it felt the presence of fear in the air. It was the grin of a predator, finally finding what it was hunting for. And Evan knew that beast would stop at nothing to get to him. The lion had indeed found the deer it had been stalking through the shadows. It opened its maw, hiding deep in the shadows, slowly creeping towards the unassuming.

With a reputation of being the most sound sleeper, the title handed over graciously by his amused mother, James had managed to not even catch a wink of sleep. After Evan had split, running into the alley like a toddler, James had gone back to his house. Even though he had initially told himself to let this issue go, it still replayed over and over in his head.

The driver of the pickup. That gruesomely broad smile. Unable to sit still, he had paced the den of his house, the place illuminated by a small lamp. God alone knew for how long he had paced, not thinking about anything in particular. Everytime James forced himself to forget about the whole thing, he kept remembering the terrified look on Evan's face.

Sure. James hadnt known the kid for a long time, but he had always felt that the kid was a tough one. And after what had happened the previous night, it was almost as if he had gotten an up-close appointment with some boogeyman.

James finally managed to get some sleep after he told himself that in the morning, he was actually going to do something about the lunatic.

Even if it may be too late by then.

ELEVEN

Howie worked thoroughly. He had learnt that from the exploits of his mother. He knew that scrubbing hot water and lemon over blood stains were often enough to remove the worst of them but he didnt have any hot water available. Nor did he have a fresh pair of clothes. Methodically, he pulled off his shirt, and held it under the stream for a few seconds. After rubbing the bloody crimson areas with the shirt itself, under water, he took it to a nearby large a smooth rock for his purpose, pounding the shirt on its surface a second time before repeating the whole process another 4 times.

Each time he walked back to the stream and to the rock, the crimson colour faded even more. There werent a lot of stains on his trousers, and he was sure that he could cover up for the ones which were there. At this moment, clothing was not his main concern. His mind was already chalking up a plan to nail Evan. Howie didnt, for the life of him, know that the man even existed. He was unsure as to why he was even going along with this plan. But yet, something deep within him told him to go ahead with it. It was the same voice, whispering in the deepest wells of his mind.

Moreover, no such person deserved to exist. No sir. And this was something the voice in his head wanted, and something told Howie that he best do what the voice said.

He didnt have any logical reason with him, but he needed none. He was going to get this Evan. One way or the other.

After going through most of the stains methodically, he hung it on a broken branch of the tree and sat and went back to the stream again. His mind was racing. The voice had told him that Evan was in this town, hiding amongst the locals, like a wolf with sheep's clothing. He desperately wanted to continue with his original plan, moving through orange county and getting all the way outta the state.

Again, he could almost imagine that voice whispering to him, flowing with knowledge, on how he'd get caught if he tried to escape. He had gotten into this way too deep. There was no going back now. If howie got caught, this time, he will be thrown behind bars of life, and no one will be able to save him by citing insanity as a reason. He wasnt a juvenile anymore. Yes. He had no other choice. He had to go through with this plan.

Only when the cloud of death isnt hanging over him, he could manage to create another plan to escape. For that he would have to do what the voice said. Howie turned, looking at the shirt hung on the branch. The large splotches of blood had dried into a deep crimson, turning the colour once blue shirt into a disgusting purplish shade. Most of the washing had managed to remove it. But the shirt wouldnt do in public. Howie desperately needed a new set of clothes.

Not to mention some more supplies, assuming he went along with his "plan". The voice murmured that there was a target around. Howie really felt uncomfortable calling his own mind a thinking "voice" but no matter how much he tried to refute those claims, he knew it wasnt just his mind.

Plucking the discoloured shirt from the branch, he pulled it on, wincing. It was fully wet. It had managed to dry a bit but it was still soaking. Setting his jaw, he moved back towards the town, careful to walk over the bushy undergrowth and protruding sticks.

The chevy was right where he had parked it the night before. He hadnt even bothered to lock it, but in such a small place, who would commit anything as grave as stealing cars? Especially when the car in question was an old beatup chevy parked under the shade of the trees?

Exactly. Howie didnt know the time. He guessed it was around a quarter to 6 AM. No doubt the usual parade of "health-conscious" people would start roaming the roads, carrying 50 phones and enough soft drinks to give a bear a caffeine-induced heart attack. Howie knew what they would think if they saw him, with his bedraggled hair and his weird looking wet shirt. He may not be mentally alright, but he wasnt stupid. He knew what they would say.

Again. Randomly accusing poor howie of something he didnt do. What did they know? Tourists. They all were gonna judge him. Judge him right to the police. Oh and what would they do? Oh yes. They would put him behind bars until the sun went out. Oh they had already tried now didnt they? Even managed to do it last time round. This time he couldnt let it happen. This time he was doing the job for something far greater than himself. He couldnt afford to get caught. Quickly, he opened the door of the chevy and got in. Howie was going for a ride.

The roads were almost mostly deserted. Howie guessed that the actual rush-hour traffic would hit the streets in another half hour. All the kids going to school and the dads and moms going to work. Howie wanted to escape the traffic. He had a busy day planned out today.

It didnt take him much time to find the nearest target, parking the chevy at the lot, he sat inside the car. He was well aware that the news about what had happened on the day before would soon be put on the news, if not already. He knew that the police would be fools not to know that he had managed to escape the county. It was common sense to set up camp in all other counties on the direction out of the state. He knew that he was bound to be caught by someone.

Howie was scared. The voice whispered again. A slow grin spread across his face. It was a grin that showed that he wasnt the headmaster and rule-by-the-looks guy. It was just the right smile to show that he was just another friendly citizen of the United States of America. No sir he wasnt responsible for a homicide. No sir. He was the type of person to smile at a barking dog. Only after carefully looking at that smile for some time would one come to know that something wasnt right with the smile. There was a slight twitch in the right side of the mouth, randomly appearing every few seconds. As if that mouth wanted to break off the leash of that ridiculous smile and do as it pleased. It suggested that the grin could go wider. And the mouth wanted the grin to go wider. A grin so wide it would be unearthly. Howie clamped his tongue under the molars, behind that curtain of a smile, and crossed the lot, heading into the store.

As if by a stroke of luck, something he hadnt seen in a while, the store was literally deserted. He racked his brain trying to remember the day. It was a tuesday. So why was there no one around? Even the front desk was deserted. It was almost as if they all had just jointly decided to not show up to work. But Howie could still see cars lined up, covering the parking lot.

So where were all the people? Howie knew it wasnt just luck. The voice in his head had somehow played a part in all this. It wasnt just a voice. It was something terribly powerful, a god ripped off his physical form. But one who, nonetheless, was just as powerful. The speakers started on their own record.

Jazz music started to flow on their own. "Thats one powerful voice in my head right there" he murmured to himself. He finally gave in to the urges of his mouth. The grin just slipped up three notches, like there was a hidden toggle controlling it.

With that unearthly grin with those burning white teeth, Howie went deeper into the store. He could buy more than a set of clothes after all.

TWELVE

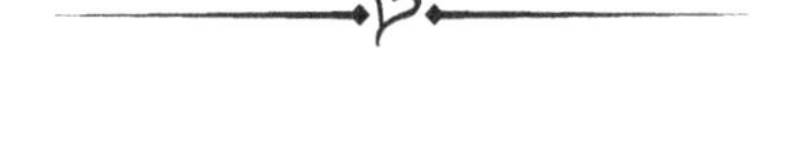

James wasnt having anything. His mind was too much of a wreck to actually even try going to work. He had spent the whole night tossing and turning, not managing to even get a wink of sleep. He knew that he probably looked like a survivor of a storm, but that was not exactly his concern right now. His concern right now was that there was a mass murderer out there somewhere, and this "somewhere" wasnt as vague as he would like it to be.

There are lunatics everywhere. It gets scary when there is one right in your backyard. James knew that Evan was hiding something from him, and that everything wasnt right with the kid. Maybe it had to do with how the kid had always skirted around when talking about his past, deftly changing topics instead of addressing them. But right now, that was not his concern right now either. He looked at the clock on the mantelpiece. It read 7 AM.

'If i knew that the kid's issue would result in a mass-murderer creeping around my place, maybe i would have been more firm about the kid's past when he tried to dodge it by ordering them extra chicken-wings with steak at dinner' James muttered to himself, pulling on a windbreaker and grabbing the keys from the bowl he kept next to the door on a table. He stood before the door of the house, keys still poised in his hand. He wondered if he really should be doing this. 'Yeah i should' he told the empty house before slamming the door shut and walking out to the crisp morning sunshine outside.

While his sentiment to "save his people" may have been valiant, Orange County was still a big place. And "his people" were roughly 3 million. The only thing that helped him was the fact that he had seen the damn psycho just waltzing in, with that smile which gave James the creeps. He broke into a medium-paced jog. If it was anything like the previous night, he would make it pretty soon.

He kept to the left, jogging under the shade of trees. The people were already out. Many of them on the way to work, some taking the time to do a jog, decked out in bright shoes and headbands. James politely went past them. His body was consciously working but still is mind was erratic. Other than going there, James had no idea what he was going there to accomplish. Well lets see, James is a 29-year old guy who works at a grocery store, with the closest he ever went to the community gym was when he had to use the restroom.

So assaulting the lunatic physically was out of the equation. He could talk to the guy. Yeah. James could talk right? Except that the person on the other side was, surprise surprise, a sociopath. That took talking out of the equation too. He sighed inwardly. He had no idea what he was gonna do. Looking downwards, he almost collided with a kid pushing his bike on the pavement, probably late to school. Muttering his apologies, he continued, his mind still wandering. He knew that he could probably be killed, and that he should call the police. He was putting himself and others in danger by not reporting the psycho to the cops.

But something told him that this wasnt the usual "im-a-killer" situation. He admittedly didnt know everything about Evans but he still cared for the kid. He was almost fully certain that this involved Evan and he didnt wanna call the cops unless he was absolutely sure of what he had seen. Which cop was gonna believe him anyway? Yeah you saw a grinning psycho at night? With only limited light? Yeah sure lets assemble an all-out manhunt for the guy just because you said so.

James told himself again. Hes not gonna do anything. Hes just gonna make sure that he saw what he saw on the previous night, then go straight to the cops. It would be Evan's decision to participate or not. But still James realized that if he reported everything that had happened, they would probably want to talk to Evan too, whether the kid wanted it or not. And the fact that he was so vague about his past told James that he might not exactly welcome the police. But he was gonna do it anyway. The first step was to just look at the lunatic.

'Just a look' he promised himself and skidded to a halt behind the same enormous and dead black escalade of god knew who, James prayed that he hadnt made a mistake. And that even if he did, he would get out of it alive.

He peeked from the side of the automobile, and looked at the spot where he thought he had seen the chevy pickup. He had seen the chevy right there, he had not mistaken. However, it occurred to him that it wasnt a total surprise to not see the pickup, standing in broad daylight. In a way he had known that the pickup wouldnt be there. A part of him had also hoped that he wouldnt see it. No murderer just parked their car on a busy street after committing a murder. That was literally common sense.

'Great' he muttered to himself, smiling for the benefit of the people jogging, giving him weird looks. He knew how it looked. He didnt care. 'Where is the damn thing' he muttered to himself again, smiling awkwardly at a couple who jogged by, looking at him. Well the chevy wasnt there. There were a few explanations. Fine. Maybe the lunatic ditched the chevy somewhere and went into hiding, deep in the forest. Psychopaths were shrewd and annoyingly cunning right? This explanation made sense. However, there was another explanation that he didnt want to go into. The explanation he didnt want to deal with was that if indeed the chevy wasnt "hidden" somewhere, then the lunatic was probably out, roaming around the streets, his eyes already prowling for the next target.

A target that could be literally anyone. A friend. A parent. A loved family member. James felt sick to his stomach again. He stepped out from behind the escalade, and looked at the opening in the forest. It was almost inviting him. Enchanting his body and soul with the thick and twisting undergrowth, shrubs and roots hiding the darkest and most lecherous beasts from mankind. He stuffed his hands in his pockets and felt the hard plastic of his phone. He really ought to call the police. But he wanted to checK. No sense in giving the Police Department a false call. No. He had to make sure that he was fully sure before he dragged everyone into this. Sure, everything didnt feel right but this was just because of the fact that James was getting cold feet. All his life he had never really done anything which was special. It was always routine, always the ordinary. Managing not to fully complete highschool., he had gone and taken up odd jobs, delivering the paper, working in the supermarket, helping people mow their lawn - it was always the routine work. There was no thrill in his life. There was no ambition. Just routine. Once he had a shot to actually do something exciting. But then he realized that this was his life that was hanging in the balance.

Ordinary or not, this was still his life. He didnt want to lose it doing something unnecessary and stupid. Yet he felt something pulling him towards the forest. Something attracting his soul. 'One quick peek and i will readily call the cops' he promised himself and quickly hurried across the street, going straight into the opening in the forest, disappearing in the thick canopy of trees and bushes.

All the while Howie sat, his eyes alight with interest. So someone had seen him yesterday. And that someone was right there, again, creeping and snooping where he didnt belong. It had taken Howie all but 15 minutes to pickout 3 pairs of inconspicuous clothes and wearing a fresh pair, discarding the old ones in the pickup. All the while the store had been empty, jazz was smoothly flowing. Howie had not been able to wipe that mad grin off his face. It hurt, but it felt good. Just after he dumped the old pair and the three new pairs of clothes carefully in the shotgun seat of the pickup, the voice- which had been almost silent until then- spoke again.

It told him about how there was someone, a stranger, snooping, hoping to catch Howie. Poor Howie, who had not done anything at all, no sir. The voice was very helpful. It told him how he should leave the pickup in the parking lot itself, yes nothing would happen to it, and he should walk right now back to the clearing in the forest where he had earlier parked his pickup. The voice promised him that if he went on time, he would get to find the snooping stranger. And now Howie stood, a good few metres away, looking intently. Maybe this stranger was that mistake of god, Evan Stevenson, himself. But howie knew that things wouldnt be that easy. No sir.

The voice assured him that it was not evan himself, but it was a fried of evan. So two people had managed to see him on the previous night. The voice had informed him that the police had already began a country-wide search for the psychopath who had killed two people before rushing from the state, but he didnt care. Howie was sure that the voice would take care of him. It was very very powerful, oh yes.

Now, he had other concerns. 'Thou shalt not steal, and thou shalt not snoop.' he muttered to himself, looking at a passing pedestrian in the eye. 'And the punishment for doing so, is death.' he told himself. His pasty and constricted face broke into a sunny grin, twitching at the sides. 'Punishment is death' he told aloud to particularly no one as he crossed the street and followed the snooping stranger into the forest. The predator was going for a hunt.

THIRTEEN

As James entered the thick canopy of the forest, it almost seemed to eat him, strangling him with overflowing shrubbery. He walked slowly, carefully placing his legs so as to not trip and fall over something. The sunlight almost seemed to be fully gone under those dense trees, in some places rendering the landscape pitch black. James felt a certain sense of unease. His mind was racing. He took several mouthfuls of the clean and crisp air in the forest, forcing himself to calm down. What's done is done. It may have been stupid, coming into this forest, but it was too late to second guess himself. He was just gonna have to go through with it. Instead of worrying, he distracted himself. He had sharp eyes. He was walking on a path, a small and narrow one.

Leaving the occasional tumbleweed of wrappers of candybars and chips, it was deserted, with almost nothing to show it had human contact at all. This further increased his sense of unease. The narrow path twisted and turned, all the while with a strict border of dense trees covering both sides of the path. He couldn't see past those dense trees. Somehow he felt certain that the chevy driver would have only gone on this path. As mentally-ill as he may be, no one was stupid enough to break a good path and rush into the trees, especially at the dead of the night, where the entre place would have no doubt been pitchblack. And if James was right, there wasn't even a moon the previous night. No. James was sure that the Chevy driver had gone in the same path. His head bent downwards, and his mind elsewhere, James followed the path. He looked forward. It appeared as if the path was opening into some sort of a clearing.

James couldn't see anything except for fierce sunshine bursting through. His heartbeat quickened. Maybe his original explanation was true. Maybe there was someone there, someone very dangerous, someone waiting. He felt scared again. Blood rushed away from his palms and feet, leaving them cold. 'Worth a shot' he muttered to himself and went ahead. As he went closer and closer to the clearing, more and more details became apparent. As he stood a few metres away from the open space of the clearing, the sunshine stinging his face, he suddenly became aware of something. He held his breath. He realized there was yet another reason for why he had felt uneasy. Why, it made so much more sense after all. He hadn't been uneasy just because he was getting cold feet and second thoughts about coming in the first place. His neck suddenly became alive, hot and itchy. A hand absently scratched his neck. Why it was because of this place. It was a forest. Yet it was dead silent. Even the chirps of birds and other sounds of animals living in the forest couldnt be heard. It was fully quiet. He could even hear his own loud breathing. Well that meant only one thing. Not a soul lived in these forests. And that included animals too.

Eddie was old and tiring. He didn't want to do these runs anymore than he had to. If his children hadn't been around, he probably wouldn't go at it, always nagging him to have some "exercise" in his life and that being 68 years old did not mean he could let his body rot. Every morning he devised clever schemes and devious excuses to escape this errand, but everyone, from his wife to his grandchild, were not to be escaped.

Well its only a matter of time before i run away from here he thought to himself. Oh how he despised doing these morning runs. Nonetheless, he jogged, slowly and steadily, his chest heaving and sweat pouring right into his eyes. He kept his head bent down as he jogged. However he just managed to look up just in time to see some guy hiding behind a black escalade, looking into a peculiar opening in the forest as if there were 100 doubloons of gold hidden there somewhere. The kids of this age he thought to himself. As he watched, the kid hurried across the street and went into the opening in the forest. What happened next was very anomalous. As soon as that guy entered the clearing in the forest, he immediately disappeared from Eddie's sight.

The kid could have even sprinted into the forest, but still, he couldn't disappear so fast right? It was almost as if as soon as the kid had stepped a foot into the forest, he had vanished. What happened next was something that Eddie hadnt seen anything like in all his 68 years of existence. As soon as the kid just about vanished, the entire forest seemed to flicker in and out, a deep purple light pulsing deep under the canopy of trees, lighting up different parts of the forest. Then, just as soon as it started, it ended. Like the boy himself, the entire forest once again pulsed, waning purple light in and out, then completely vanishing too, leaving behind an empty plot of land. Eddie stopped dead in his tracks, his mouth in a small O of wonder. His chest was still heaving and his heart was still steadily pumping blood to all his weakened limbs. He just stood there, dumbstruck, as he looked at the empty plot of land where once there had been a forest. Other pedestrians walked by as if nothing had happened.

Eddie racked his brain, trying to remember if he had seen the forest before on other runs, but his mind kept failing him. As he stood there, stupidly staring at an empty plot of land, a man walked past him, dressed in a brown shirt and cargo shorts, this queer attire complete with navy blue flipflops. Eddie didn't have a chance to look at the man's face. However, that smell which came off that man was enough for Eddie to refocus his mind. He felt nauseous. The smell of dead rats still welcomed his nostrils. Eddie looked at the man, navy blue flip-flops and an uneven haircut. Almost as if the guy had decided to cut his hair at home and had taken a trimmer to task, diligently cutting off his hair in the front, in uniform motions. Then suddenly as he had reached the back part of his head, he had taken the trimmer in wild twists and loops, leaving queer slashes of hair trimmed and other parts not trimmed. Like the man had decided that he could only properly see the front part of his hair so that was the only part that mattered. The guy was going to be the stuff of nightmares for any barber.

As Eddie watched, the guy in the freaky haircut went towards the open plot of land, seemingly where the opening to the forest had been. As soon as that guy stepped foot in the open plot, the forest appeared again, flickering in and out, constantly moving, as if it was the screen of some moving projector. Eddie froze again. As the man entered the forest, he turned back to look at Eddie, winking with muddy and bloodshot eyes before vanishing fully from sight. Again, no other pedestrian seemed to care, all engrossed in their own life. With a start Eddie realized that he had been holding in his breath for all this time. He had to go and see it too. He had to. Just when he took the first few steps towards the empty plot of clearing, a voice whispered in his head. It was smooth and melodious, murmuring honey-sweet words in his head. A slow dazed smile spread across his face.

Yes. He didn't need to go to the forest afterall. Yes. He was perfectly fine with finishing his run and going back home. Yes. He would totally forget what had happened today and what he had seen. No sir. He definitely not report this as a mystery to any single living soul. Yes sir he would take this to his grave. That dazed smile still plastered across his face, Eddie Halloway completed his run and went home. What had happened that day was instantly forgotten, hidden deep beneath ages' worth of memories and knowledge. He had completely forgotten what had happened that day. It had just been another simple day hasn't it? Yes sir. No. This memory never came back when he was awake. However, this always came back in his deepest and darkest nightmares, rattling him and making him wake up, bolt upright, at 2 AM in the morning, his pyjama shirt fully wet from sweat. He drank a cup of water and went back to sleep.

By the time he woke up in the morning and went about to do his errands, it was fully forgotten yet again

FOURTEEN

Howie was watching the guy from a good 100 metres behind, his rheumy and bloodshot eyes staring at the guy. The guy who had seen him yesterday. The guy who had now come for him. The snoop. The snooping snoop. 'Coming here to put me back' he muttered to himself, his fists clenched hard. 'Not this time buckaroo' he muttered to himself again, watching with growing eagerness as the guy looked around himself, crossing the road and heading towards the forest. The forest which was not a forest. No it wasn't confusing. Well, not confusing...anymore. Initially, Howie had been sceptical of the voice in his head, because all he could see there when he first laid eyes was a patch of barren land. The voice persuaded him, telling him, the moment he stepped foot into that patch of land, the entire earth would surround him, protecting him from everyone.

Everyone who wanted desperately to throw poor howie behind bars. Just like they did to his mother. Listening to the voice, Howie had stepped foot into the patch of land, and immediately, as if it were magic, trees erupted from the ground, growing to full length until he was surrounded by dense foliage. It was almost as if it was magic. But howie knew better. Magic isn't real. It never existed. The ones who claimed were either looking to make a quick buck, or had witnessed something which they shouldn't have been a part of. This was the power of the voice in his head. The voice was not something his imagination had just created, as Howie had initially feared, but was a mere extension of a creature far more powerful. Howie was happy. Because right now, this creature was going to grant him everything he ever wanted in his life.

Howie deftly followed the kid stepping into the forest. Just as the kid placed a foot in the forest, the form of the forest flickered, pulsing in and out of sight, before regaining its original and crisp image. Howie smiled to himself as he watched an old man, with neon blue running shoes, looking at the forest, his mouth open and his eyes wide and unblinking. 'First time eh?' he thought to himself, smirking to himself as he walked past the old man and himself stepped into the forest. As soon as he stepped foot into the forest, he felt a jolt of adrenaline, pumping throughout his body.

It was like he had just gotten his body set up to a huge battery. He knew why he had a burst of energy. The voice was home. And since it was now basically a part of his own body, he was home. Howie was home. And what do you do when some intruder breaks into your home? Yes. You make sure that they regret ever being born. Howie smiled to himself again, going off the path, going deeper and deeper into the thick canopy of rustling trees. He was just taking a shortcut.

FIFTEEN

James was still standing at the end of the path, squinting against the bright sunlight which was coming from the wide clearing. James' heart was hammering in his chest. He knew that one way or the other, one of his explanations was going to get verified. Either he was going to go face-to-face with the killer, or was just going to feel stupid after hyping himself up for an empty plot of land. Taking in a deep breath, he walked forward into the sunlight, his hands tightly clenched into fists, at his sides. As soon as he stepped into the clearing, he was aware of the sudden change in the flooring. The ground here seemed more lower, the mud squelching under his boots as he stepped away from the path on the grass. He took in another deep breath.

Walking deeper into the open land, he looked around himself in awe. It seemed that he was in the heart of the forest itself. Unimaginably humongous trees stretched as far as the eye could see, the branches of these trees growing upward, its tips looking like gnarled fingers pointing up at the sky. The air here smelled fresh and pure, James eager to take in lungfuls of it. He looked down and was jolted back to reality. A set of muddy footprints were visible in the green grass, heading ahead. In his wonder about how such a secluded place existed while steadily the town around it expressed more ambition about being developed and a metropolitan city, he had forgotten about the main reason that he had been led here.

The lunatic. He bent down and touched the muddy footprints. He had no method to determine if it had been recent or not. Still, something was better than nothing. He bent his head down and followed the muddy footprints, going deeper and deeper into the forest, away from the clearing and once more deep into the trees. Even though he was surrounded by a thick canopy of trees, he could clearly make out the footprints, which seemed undisturbed and fresh. While his body walked on, his mind wandered. He was still thinking about how deep the chevy driver could have gone when he heard the sound of running water. Excited, he picked up his pace, jogging along, following the steps. He hurried, leaping over fallen logs and branches, his eyes on the footsteps.

He was following no path. He was just following footprints leading deeper into the forest. He emerged from the trees, into a small ledge of land, a few metres away from a small but fast-flowing stream of water, cutting its way across the deep forest. The footsteps were missing now. They had stopped in the forest, the last pair in front of a protruding tree. James into the small ledge of land. The stream was wide enough for 3 people to get in, side by side, but James guessed that it wasn't very deep. The water was flowing fast. It cut the forest, a path visible on the other side of the stream. James had no idea of whether or not the footprints continued on the other side of the stream. As he looked into the stream to judge its depth, he heard a loud crunching sound towards the trees on his right. James sharply looked in that direction, his body suddenly very alert. He felt like a deer, a vulnerable creature just minding its business in a deep foliage, ready to run at any time a predator decided to make its appearance visible.

James was feeling watched. He shook himself, mentally scolding himself to stop being spooked over nothing. He tried into the shadows of the trees to his right, and suddenly felt as if there was someone standing there, looking over at him, calmly waiting for his opportunity to strike. James shook himself again. It was probably nothing. Just a couple of shadows is all. As he turned his head back to the stream to check its depth, he suddenly stopped. His eyes widened. He remembered how the entire forest had been dead quiet, and he had concluded to himself that there must be no wildlife present in these trees, but then what had made the crunching sound? Maybe there had been some animal which had made the sound, since it was impossible to make out if there were any animals in such a vast forest. Maybe there was some animal hidden which he had seen. Anyway, James was suddenly tired of trying to find the Chevy driver. He would just go to the police. No fuss. He lifted his head, meaning to turn away from the stream and head back where he had started when he felt a whoosh of air near his right ear.

He just had time to half turn before some heavy object crashed hard into the side of his head, his knees involuntarily locking, sending him sprawling on the soft and coarse soil in the sides of the stream. He landed on his palms, pain blasting through his entire head, as his blood started flowing down the side of his head, dripping downwards. James wasn't even able to see his attacker. There was a grunt as James felt another heavy strike of the object on his back, battering his spinal cord, right at the centre. Pain exploded through his back, the pain in his face temporarily forgotten.

His elbows collapsed at the sudden blow to his back, sending him falling face-down on the soil, on the side of his face where he had been struck earlier. He could almost feel the hot steel rods of pain tumbling through the lower part of his body. His hands fell at either sides of his body, the air sucked out of his body. James struggled to breathe, his open mouth gasping like he was a fish out of water. All of this happened within mere seconds.

Outstretched palms made weak fists in the soil, teetering on the edge of unconsciousness. His body suddenly felt distant and far away, as if James himself was watching what was happening to his body a few hundred metres above, away from the pain. A flurry of blows landed on his back, none of which he was able to feel. Oddly enough,a tiny smile cracked from his upturned and bloody mouth, his white teeth visible through his parched lips. James thought he heard a loud howl.

Though at that point, it was hard to say if it was a howl or a wail. Then again, what difference did any of it make? Grinning to himself, James slipped out of consciousness.

SIXTEEN

Evan checked his watch again. It was 7:30. The usual crowd of customers had already started to file in, carrying their big bags of groceries and other essentials. Something wasnt right. James was one of the most regular guys who worked there, coming every morning at 7 AM. It was actually entertaining for the other guys as they had bets amongst themselves if James would even be a minute late. The man was the clock. 7 AM meant 7 AM. Not 7:01 and not 6:59. It was also something that gave him a lot of respect from the others, including the supervisor, who was a person no human on Earth was able to satisfy completely. Evan checked his watch again, sighing. So what if he was half an hour late? So what if he didnt come at all? After what they both had seen yesterday, any sane person wouldnt come to work at all. Thats all it is. Maybe james just needs some time to process what he had seen and what he should do about it.

Evan had explicitly made it clear to James that the police was not to be a part of anything. Evan had been hanging around here for the past 6 years, and actually, he kinda liked it here. The neighbours were helpful, the place wasnt clogged with traffic, and most importantly, the people just didnt care that much about you to notice that a guy looked the same for the past 6 years. Sure, he had done a lot of odd jobs but the fact that he still hadnt been recognized was extraordinary. The chevy driver really bugged him. It was gnawing at his skull. He knew he should be doing something but for the life of him, didnt know what to do. All Evan knew was that this was not the first time he had encountered someone like this. From the first time Evan laid eyes on the lunatic, he knew that he was discovered. Somehow, the chevy driver knew all about him.

Evan could feel it. He knew that he had to take care of this lunatic before the authorities got involved. He sighed again. The thought of running away from Orange County altogether did go through his mind, but he couldnt do that. Not after everything the people had done, though unknowingly. This was the longest he was able to stay in one place without being discovered for who he truly was. Evan wasnt an idiot. He knew that some people were beginnign to notice him, thinking how odd it was that the "kid" always looked the same, almost as if the kid never aged, but for most of the people, this was still an involuntary observation. It was still something that they were unsure of.

Something they kid to themselves before they fell asleep. Something that could be thought about but never be spoken out loud because once something like this is spoken out loud, it suddenly becomes real and open to the people who listen. It isnt something which is just one of those fantasy daydreams. It becomes real. And at this point, no one really noticed that much to tell it out loud. This meant that Evan was running on less time. He had to do something about the lunatic who had strolled into town...before leaving the town for good.

Evan decided enough was enough. He took off his cap and apron, putting it at the small stool which served as his seat and looking toward the manager's room before grabbing his bag and heading out. The other employees stared open-mouthed as Evan just headed out.

James lived in a small apartment close to supermarket. Even though Evan hadnt actually gone there himself, he had an idea on where it was. Jogging, his windbreaker clutched tightly in his right fist, he made his way to the small apartment. He climbed up the stairs, taking two at a time, before he reached the second floor. Each floor had only 5 apartments, spread out on either side in a long corridor. He went to the appropriate flat and rapped at the wooden door with his knuckles. He tried knocking 4 more times. Something wasnt right. James wasnt at work and nor was he at his house.

Where else could he have gone? Evan took a deep breathe and asked himself to calm down. There were other perfectly logical reasons for where james might be. Afterall, the man had witnessed something downright horrendous on the night before. Maybe he hadnt wanted to stay at his house. Maybe he had gone out for a walk. Maybe he was staying in a hotel room. Maybe he had fled the state. Or maybe, even after Evan had explicitly forbidden it, the guy had gone to the police. It was all very possible. Evan sighed again. He wasnt feeling well about this.

He banged the door with the palms of his hand out of sheer desperation, the act giving no response except for the old door to rattle in its hinges. His head bent down, he lumbered down the stairs, walking down to the street. Dejected, he looked around at either sides, suddenly picking up an idea. Evan didnt know why this thought had occurred to him , and at the moment, he didnt particularly care. His eyes widened. There was no logic behind what he was thinking, it was intuition.

He somehow *knew* where his old friend might be. Absent-mindedly, stuffing his phone in his back pocket, he started jogging towards the direction of the grove where they had seen that damn chevy, with which so much of his troubles had started.

SEVENTEEN

James felt a deep throb in his head. His consciousness was swimming and swirling, unable to focus. Random thoughts popped in his head like firecrackers, like what he had eaten for breakfast, even though he hadnt eaten any that day. The pain in his head pulsed, as if someone was repeatedly striking his skull with a jackhammer. He tried to open his eyes a few times, failing each time as his eyelids refused to open. Finally, on god knew which attempt, he managed to open his eyes, owlishly blinking. If not for that piercing pain in his head, he may as well just gone asleep for sometime. He opened his eyes fully, squinting against the harsh morning sunlight.

He turned his head around, the tendons in his neck creaking. He looked down and saw with a weary sort of amusement at the bundles of rope tied in a haphazard manner, cris-crossing all over his chest. He even grinned to himself. He flexed his fingers, feeling it tied tauntly behind his back. He sighed. He managed to look up to see a figure standing at a distance from him, his back facing James. Somehow James had concluded to himself that the figure was a "he". *Jamieee'* a soft voice called out in his head. James jerked. He was fully alert now.

He hadnt heard anyone call him that for a long time. *'Heyo Jamie'* the voice whispered again, creeping up through the clogged pipes of his mind. James wanted to yell out. Fight. To do *something. Anything.* But he couldnt. He just sat there, jerking randomly as if he were sitting on a nest of ants. The figure wanted his attention. Well, now it had it. It continued whispering, and James listened.

Evan was jogging at a medium pace when his phone began to ring. Initially, he was too distracted to even pay attention to it, only later realizing that it was ringing. He slowed down to a walk and pulled out his flip phone from his backpocket.

It was an unknown number. Evan frowned. He had only gotten a phone 2 weeks before, he really was tired of all the shocked glances that everyone gave him when he told them he didnt have a phone. He pushed 'accept' and pulled the phone to his ear, ready to dismiss the call and get back to jogging his way to the grove. What he heard made him dead stop in his tracks. A voice cut through the crackle of his phone.

'Evan' a voice called out. 'Listen to me and listen close. Come to the grove. Im tied up here.' and before Evan could even respond, the line went dead. He called back again, knowing full well that there wouldnt be any response from the other side. He knew what was happening. He was being set-up. But he didnt exactly have any other choice. He had to save James, whether he was walking into a trap or not. James was in this mess because of him. While virtually nothing had happened in the past two days when this whole mess had started, it wasnt about the past two days. It was about the decades worth of struggle to either side. Evan shouldnt be alive. He knew it. *They* knew it.

With a sinking feeling, Evan started running faster towards the grove. Something told him that this time was going to be different. This wasnt the usual. He had managed to escape death for centuries now, but it had taken its toll. He made up his mind. If there indeed came a choice between his own life and james' he would happily give his away.

'Living forever does suck though' he muttered to himself pushing himself to run faster.

EIGHTEEN

Evan managed to get there soon enough. He absently noted how the grove was flickering and whooshing, as if it was the light of a cheap projector on a torn bedsheet. He walked right into it, not bothering to even look at the ground as he sprinted faster, breath whooshing down his lungs. Straight ahead, he could see a clearing, with sunlight blasting through.

The light at the end of the tunnel he thought to himself as he neared it. Without halting, he jumped from the footwalk to the clearing. He landed on wet grass, his shoes sliding off the surface of the earth. He managed to keep his balance for about two seconds before he tumbled and fell, falling on his elbows and knees. Rolling over, he stood, his jaw clenched and his eyes searching. He almost immediately saw what he was looking for. On the trunk of an enormous was James, his figure slumped, with bundles and bundles of rope tied all around his chest and legs. Evan felt anger building up in him. He had been chased for a very long time now. He was tired and angry. He was done running. He turned his head to the right, noticing for the first time to small stream which was flowing. On its bank stood another figure, its back against Evan. Well, who else could it be? His hands balled up into tight fists on the sides of him, he yelled at the figure. It came out as a loud and hoarse cry, his heart still racing.

He saw the figure bending its head, its neck shifting. *'Tell me....are you ready to pay for your sins?'* a voice as cold as ice flashed through his mind. He was disoriented but his anger was still rising. This was not his fault. He hadnt *asked* to live forever among these beasts which call themselves humans. He had to witness the death of everyone he had ever held dear. He had to be constantly on the run, hiding his true identity, always scared if whether they would find out. He had lost all the joys in his life, until it had become a nightmare. He hadnt *asked* for any of this. He was given this. He was chosen.

And he sure was not going to let anyone take that away from him, least of all a demon with a grudge on him. He had been chosen for a reason. Evan didnt exactly know what that reason was, and he guessed that he never will. It was faith. Thats all it ever was. No one had *any* idea of what they were capable of, vast reservoirs of untapped potential just lying around. *'redemption as arrived. Its time that this...mistake is fixed.'* the voice whispered.

In his reamarkably long life, Evan had seen millions of people with staggering potential and energy, let it all go down the drain as they never truly realised what they were meant to be. A god was not someone who lived forever, but was someone who fully knew his identity. They had a vast ocean waiting for them, and they contented themselves with a dip in the kiddie pool. Well, maybe it was time for some redemption. Evan grinned to himself. Walking towards the figure with its back turned on him. It was time to set things right. One way or the other, only one would walk out of this alive. Still grinning, he broke into a full sprint at the figure as it turned around towards him.

Evan was tired of the kiddie pool. He was going for the ocean.